This book belongs to:

. . . .

. . . .

Editor: Carly Madden
Designer: Hannah Mason
Series Designer: Rachel Lawston
Editorial Director: Victoria Garrard
Art Director: Laura Roberts-Jensen

Copyright © QED Publishing 2015
First published in the UK in 2015
by QED Publishing
Part of The Quarto Group
The Old Brewery
6 Blundell Street
London N7 9BH
www.qed-publishing.co.uk

A catalogue record for this book is available from the British Library.

ISBN 978 1 78493 122 3

Printed in China

Don't Pick Your Nose, Pinocchio!

Written by Steve Smallman
Illustrated by Neil Price

Geppetto was a carpenter.

He had no family and was very lonely. He decided to make himself a wooden puppet boy and pretend that it was his son.

The puppet was very realistic.
It even had nostrils!

Geppetto called him Pinocchio.

Geppetto talked to
Pinocchio all the time.

But Pinocchio
couldn't talk back.

Geppetto got some
very strange looks
when people saw them
out together.

Then one day,
a kind-hearted fairy
waved her wand and...

POOOOOOF!

...Pinocchio came to life!

"Be a good son to Geppetto," the fairy told him.

"Don't tell lies, don't pick your nose and one day you'll be a real boy!"

Pinocchio tried very hard to be good,
but he couldn't resist sticking
his finger up his nose and
rummaging about.

He pulled out little
wooden bogies and flicked
them across the floor.

Geppetto slipped on them and fell with a bump!

"Pinocchio!" he shouted.

"Have you been picking your nose?"

"Pinocchio, have you been **picking your nose?**" asked Geppetto again.

"Er... yes, Father,"

said Pinocchio and his nose shrank back to normal.

One day Pinocchio was
playing under the kitchen table.

"Are you picking your
nose, Pinocchio?"
called Geppetto.

"No, Father!"
called Pinocchio.

Poiiiiing!

Pinocchio still had his finger stuck up his
nostril when his nose grew. It grew so quickly that
his arm came off, and shot across the room!

Geppetto mended Pinocchio's arm,
then he fetched a little box
and opened it up.

"Pinocchio," he said.
"Meet **Mr Cricket**.
He's going to stay with
you and help you stop
picking your nose."

Pinocchio's nose started to tickle but as he lifted up his finger Mr Cricket hopped onto it and shouted,

"DON'T PICK YOUR NOSE, PINOCCHIO!"

So he didn't!

Then Mr Cricket played games with Pinocchio to keep his fingers busy.

But one day, Mr Cricket jumped onto Pinocchio's finger just too late and got shoved right up his nose!

"Get me out!" he cried.

"HOW?" asked Pinocchio.

"Blow your nose into a tissue!" said Mr Cricket.

So Pinocchio
blew his nose and...

POP!

POP!

...out came Mr Cricket!

"I'm so sorry, Mr Cricket,"
said Pinocchio.

"I promise I'll try not to
pick my nose any more.
Blowing it is much more fun!"

The fairy had been watching and was so pleased with Pinocchio that...

POOF!

...she turned him into a real boy!

And from that day, Pinocchio never ever picked his nose again.

Next steps

Show the children the cover again. When they first saw it, did they think that they already knew the story? How is this story different from the traditional story? Which bits are the same?

Pinocchio's nose grew longer whenever he told a lie. Ask the children to pretend to be Pinocchio. Then ask them some silly questions that they can 'lie' about. For example, are you an elephant? Do you live on the moon? If they say 'yes', make them pretend that their noses are growing, using the 'Poiiiing!' noise.

The kind-hearted fairy told Pinocchio not to pick his nose. Why did she say that? Is it a bad thing to pick your nose? Ask the children if they ever pick their noses. Mr Cricket tried hard to help Pinocchio to stop picking his nose. What did he do?

What happened when Mr Cricket hopped onto Pinocchio's finger too late? How did Pinocchio get Mr Cricket out of his nose? What did that teach Pinocchio?

Ask the children to draw a picture of Pinocchio's face and help them to cut a slot where the nose should be. Draw a very long nose on another piece of paper, cut it out, push it through the slot and watch Pinocchio's nose grow!